The books in the Here's Hank series are designed using the font Dyslexie. A Dutch graphic designer and dyslexic, Christian Boer, developed the font specifically for dyslexic readers. It's designed to make letters more distinct from one another and to keep them tied down, so to speak, so that the readers are less likely to flip them in their minds. The letters in the font are also spaced wide apart to make reading them easier.

Dyslexie has characteristics that make it easier for people with dyslexia to distinguish (and not jumble, invert, or flip) individual letters, such as: heavier bottoms (b, d), larger than normal openings (c, e), and longer ascenders and descenders (f, h, p).

This fun-looking font will help all kids—not just those who are dyslexic—read faster, more easily, and with fewer errors. If you want to know more about the Dyslexie font, please visit the site www.dyslexiefont.com.

CHAPTER 1

"I have a great idea," I said to my best friends, Frankie Townsend and Ashley Wong. "After school today, let's put on a worm race. Not just any worm race. The First-Ever Hank Zipzer Uphill Worm Sprint."

It was Taco Tuesday, and we were in our school lunchroom eating—you guessed it—tacos. I like mine with no onions.

"Two problems," Frankie said, his mouth full of cheese and

beans. "Number one: Worms are slow and slimy."

"Yeah," Ashley agreed. "It's so gross when they leave that icky slime trail."

"No, slime is good," I said. "The trail will give us proof of which worm crosses the finish line first."

"Okay, Zip, I'll give you that," Frankie said. "But we still have problem number two. Where are we going to find these speedy worms?"

"I've got that solved," I said. "I saw three of them sticking their heads out of the dirt in the planter in front of our building this morning. They were practically begging me to let them race. I bet they'll be there after school."

Ashley and Frankie gave each other a weird look.

"Actually, Hank," Ashley said slowly. "Frankie and I are busy after school today."

"Busy doing what? The three of us always do an after-school activity together."

"Listen, Zip," Frankie said, putting his hot-sauce-covered hand on my shoulder. "Ashley and I have been asked to be on the second-grade basketball team. The one that's going to play PS 91 in our yearly game."

That totally took me by surprise.

"Really?" I said. "How come I didn't hear about this?"

Ashley pushed her sparkly purple glasses up on her nose.

"Well," she said, "they only asked the kids who are really good at basketball in gym class. Anyone else who wants to be on the team can come to tryouts. There are still some open spots."

I was quiet as her words bounced around in my brain like a Ping-Pong ball. Frankie knew what I was thinking.

"Hey, don't feel bad, Zip," he said. "They only asked certain kids because this is a really important game. Our school has beaten PS 91 two years in a row. If we win this year, it will be a three-peat. The first three-peat ever in the whole history of PS 87!"

"But I want to play, too," I said. "It says right on my report card that I play well with others."

"You sure do, Zip. But you have to admit, you're not that great at basketball."

"What exactly are you saying, Frankie? That I'm short?"

"No, that's not it," Frankie said. "Look at Ashley. She's short and she's on the team."

Ouch, that hurt.

"I'm not short," Ashley said. "I like to think of myself as vertically challenged."

"Me too," I said. "I'm going to ask the coach if I can try out."

"Why not?" Ashley said. "It never hurts to try. If you don't, you'll never know."

"Okay, I'm going to do it. By the way, who is the coach?"

"Ms. Adolf," Ashley said, "the fourth-grade teacher."

I felt my throat tighten up, then the rest of my body followed.

"You mean the one who looks like she swallowed a lemon?" I squeaked.

"Yup," Frankie answered. "Old sourpuss herself."

That wasn't what I wanted to hear. It was hard enough to ask to be on a team that nobody wanted you on. But now I was going to have to ask the meanest teacher on the whole planet Earth. Just looking at Ms. Adolf scared me down to my bones. Her hair was gray. Her clothes were gray. Her face was gray. Even her breath was gray.

"Hey, look," Ashley said, pointing across the room. "Ms. Adolf is on lunch patrol. She's standing over there by the desserts, making sure no one takes one."

"Go talk to her now, Zip,"
Frankie said, giving me a push.
"Tell her you want to be on
the team."

I got to my feet, walked over
to Ms. Adolf, and gave her my
best Zipzer smile. She did not
smile back.

"Don't even think about
taking one of these desserts,"
she barked at me. "It will rot

your teeth and ruin your brain."

"Actually, Ms. Adolf, I'm here to talk basketball. I'd like to try out for the second-grade team that you're coaching."

She pulled her gray glasses down on her gray nose and stared at me like I was a flea that just fell off a dog.

"Can you shoot?" she asked.

"No."

"Can you rebound?"

"No."

"Can you jump high?"

"No."

"Can you dribble?"

"Only from my mouth," I said. Then I cracked up. But not Ms. Adolf. She just sighed heavily.

"There will be an open tryout this afternoon at three, in the gym," she said. "I've already selected four players for the team. But I can add five more to round out the roster. You can come then, but don't get your hopes up."

"Great, I'll be there," I said.

"You'll see. I'm going to surprise you."

As I walked away, I felt pretty good, and my hopes were up . . . until I suddenly realized that I had nothing to surprise her with. Not one thing.

I had to come up with something. And fast.

CHAPTER 2

FOUR WAYS I COULD SURPRISE MS. ADOLF AT BASKETBALL TRYOUTS

BY HANK ZIPZER

1. I could arrive in a full bunny suit with ears and a fluffy cottontail. (This has nothing to do with basketball, but boy, would that surprise Ms. Adolf.)

2. I could buy two tiny ladders and tie them to the bottom of my feet to make myself taller. (That would surprise everyone, including me, because there's no such thing as a tiny-ladder store.)

3. I could make ten slam dunks in a row. (Not only would that surprise Ms. Adolf, it would surprise the entire solar system, including everybody on Neptune.)

4. There is no number four. Sorry, I'm not good at counting.

CHAPTER 3

After school, I hurried to the gym. I thought that being the first one at tryouts would impress Ms. Adolf. Maybe I couldn't dribble, but at least I could be on time.

When I was halfway down the hall, I realized that my body felt awfully light. I looked over my shoulder and noticed that my backpack straps were missing. So was my backpack.

I spun around and sprinted back to class. When I reached the door, my teacher, Ms. Flowers, was standing there holding my backpack out in front of her. She knows me so well.

"Forget something?" she asked with a smile.

"Thanks, Ms. Flowers," I said, taking the backpack and flinging it over my shoulder.

"By the way, Hank," she whispered. "Did you know your backpack smells strongly of pickles?"

"Yeah, isn't it great? I sprinkle a little pickle juice in there sometimes, just to keep my nose happy."

"You're an interesting boy," she said.

"Thanks again," I shouted as I took off down the hall.

When I got to the gym, I flew through the door. Unfortunately, Ms. Adolf was standing right in front of it, and I ran smack into her.

She didn't exactly fall down, but she stumbled forward a few steps, which made her blow her whistle really loud. The whole gym got quiet, waiting to see how mad she was going to get.

She got pretty mad.

"Of course it's you, Henry," she said, squinting at me with her beady gray eyes.

"I'm sorry, Ms. Adolf. I didn't mean to knock you over."

"But you did," she said. "Everyone else seems to have gotten here without creating an accident. And what is that terrible pickle odor?"

"Garlic dills," I answered. "They're my favorite."

"Perhaps you and your pickles can stand farther away," she said, holding her nose.

I took a few steps back. It was then I noticed that Ms. Adolf was wearing shorts.

My eyes almost popped out of my head. She isn't the kind of person who wears shorts. Her bony gray knees looked like they had never seen daylight before.

I looked around the room. Frankie and Ashley were sitting in the bleachers, and next to them were Heather Payne and Nick McKelty. There were five other second-graders waiting to try out for the team, just like me.

"Based on their excellent performance in gym class, I have already chosen the following students for our team," Ms. Adolf said, reading from a clipboard. "Frankie Townsend, Ashley Wong, Heather Payne, and Nick McKelty."

Nick McKelty! Why would anyone choose Nick the Tick? That guy moves like a dump truck. And besides, he's the worst sport in the world. Maybe he got picked because his head looks like a basketball, only with teeth.

"Today, I will pick five more players to complete our team," Ms. Adolf said. "One to play on the main team, and the other four will serve as backup on the bench."

"I'm really good at backing up," I said with a big smile. "I can walk backward from Ms. Flowers's classroom all the way to the water fountain."

Everyone in the bleachers howled. Well, everyone except

McKelty. Even though I didn't mean to be funny, it sure felt good hearing them laugh.

"As usual, Henry, you have misunderstood," Ms. Adolf snarled. "I'm asking you to sit on the bench as a backup player who goes in the game when we need a substitute."

"But I don't want to be a substitute, I want to be one of the main guys."

"In that case," Ms. Adolf said, "you may try out first. Let's see if you qualify. I want you to pick up the basketball, dribble from one end of the court to the other, and when you get to the basket, shoot."

"No problem," I said, tossing my backpack on the floor.

Frankie got up from the bleachers and handed me a basketball.

"Stay calm, Zip," he whispered in my ear. "Focus. You can do this."

I took the ball and walked to the end of the court. When I turned around and looked up at the basket, it seemed like it was miles away.

On the one hand, that was bad.
On the other hand, that was really
bad. But I told myself that if I
just used the old Zipzer attitude,
I could do it.

I took a deep breath and
bounced the ball. To my surprise,
it came right back to the palm
of my hand. Hey, this wasn't so
hard. I took a few more steps and
bounced the ball again. There it
was, right back in my hand.

Look at me, world,
I'm dribbling!

Oh wait, don't
look at me now,
world!

Suddenly, the
ball left my hand

and took off like it had a mind
of its own. It rolled all the way
across the court, without me
attached. I glanced over at Ashley.
She was covering her eyes.

"Hey, butterfingers," Nick
McKelty shouted from the
bleachers. "You call that
basketball? I call it bowling."

Then he let out one of his
rhinoceros snorts.

I raced across the court and picked up the ball, flashed a smile like I had meant to drop the ball, and went back to the center of the court. As I started to dribble again, I noticed that Ms. Adolf was writing something down on her clipboard. I was pretty sure she was not writing "Excellent job."

I tried the dribbling thing four more times. One time I dribbled the ball on my toe. Another time it just stopped dead on the floor in front of me. And you don't even want to know about the two times I fell on my butt. Finally, I picked up the ball and ran across the court to the net.

*There are
a lot of ways to
get to the net,*
I thought. *And
this is my way.*

I stared up
at the basket. It
seemed higher than
I imagined. I took aim,
bent my knees, and
pushed the ball with all my might
up into the air. Wow, it went
high. It sailed up into a perfect
arc. It was a pretty good shot,
if I do say so myself.

Too bad it didn't go anywhere
near the basket. It seemed to
take a left turn somewhere near
Ms. Adolf's head. She ducked,

but not enough. The ball
bounced off the back of her
head, flattening her gray bun
like a pancake.

Oops.

Something told me this was
not the best way to make the
team.

CHAPTER 4

When I was finished, I sat down in the bleachers and watched the rest of the kids try out.

The next two kids were very impressive. Ryan Shimozato sunk his first basket. It didn't even touch the rim, just went straight in. When it was Luke Whitman's turn, he managed to make a basket while picking his nose. That's not easy to do. Katie Sperling went next. She demanded that they wash the ball with soap and water before she'd touch it. That must have worked, because she made a basket, too.

Samir Patel tried a fancy dribble, but it backfired and hit him in the nose. Kim Paulson tried out in her ballet tutu because she had a dance rehearsal right after tryouts. Every time she dribbled the ball, she did a ballet leap across the floor. We thought she was showing off, but Ms. Adolf lapped it up.

Once everyone had his or her turn, Ms. Adolf told us all to line up on the court. As I watched her looking down at her clipboard, I got really nervous. She was taking her time, and every second that went by made me even more jumpy. It's a good thing I was standing in between Frankie and Ashley, or I would have bounced out of my skin.

I didn't even notice when Principal Love walked into the gym.

"Well, what kind of gathering do we have here? Something sports-related, I presume," he said.

"It's basketball tryouts," Ashley answered.

"Ah, yes! That would explain why Ms. Adolf is wearing shorts."

Ms. Adolf gave him a nasty stare.

"Excuse me, Principal Love," she said. "I was just about to announce who made the second-grade team that will compete against PS 91."

"Go right ahead," he said. "I'd love to meet the team. There is nothing more thrilling than watching a team be a team, participating in teamwork."

Don't get upset if you didn't understand that sentence. No one understands Principal Love when he talks. We just watch his lips move until he's done.

"Will the following students please step forward," Ms. Adolf said. "Frankie, Ashley, Nick, Heather, and Katie. These are the children who will make up our first-string team."

I was glad for them. Well, to be honest, I wasn't that glad for Nick McKelty, but I was truly happy for the others. I knew I wasn't a starter. But I crossed my fingers behind my back, hoping that I could at least be a

substitute. All I wanted was to be a member of the team.

"I'd like the following students to step forward now," I heard Ms. Adolf say. "You will be our substitute players, a very important part of the team. Kim Paulson, Ryan Shimozato, and Luke Whitman. Luke, please keep your fingers out of your nose when you're playing."

The three kids stepped forward. There was only one place left. I crossed my fingers so hard, I couldn't feel the tips.

Please! Let her pick me!

"The last person," Ms. Adolf said, "is Samir Patel."

Samir stepped forward to join

the other three. That left me, only me, standing by myself in the back row. I could feel the tears wanting to shoot down my cheeks. I was barely able to hold them back.

"Excuse me, Ms. Adolf," Principal Love said, walking up right next to her. "You can't leave one child out."

"That child is completely

unskilled in basketball," she answered, pointing at me.

"I'm sure you will find some appropriate role for him on the team," Principal Love said. "Even the smallest ant can carry one hundred times its own body weight."

Actually, my sister, Emily, who loves reptiles and insects, says that some ants can carry five thousand times their body weight. I didn't think this was a good time to correct Principal Love's science facts, though. I still had no idea why he brought up ants in the first place. But I was so happy he did, because it seemed to change Ms. Adolf's mind.

"Fine," she said. At least, that's what her mouth said. Her face said the opposite. "Hank Zipzer, you may step forward."

I took a big step and joined the other kids in line.

I'd made it! I was on the team.

"Practice begins tomorrow at three o'clock," Ms. Adolf said. "Be prompt. Be focused. And no gum chewing during practice."

I was so glad to have been chosen. I made a promise to myself: I was going to be prompt. I was going to be focused. And I was going to be gumless.

CHAPTER 5

"I made the basketball team," I blurted out at the dinner table that night.

"Hank, you interrupted your sister," my mom said. "She was just telling us about what happens to reptiles in cold weather."

"I'm sorry, Emily," I said, although I didn't really mean it. "I just couldn't keep the good news in my body anymore. So it flew off my tongue."

"Hank, I didn't know you had an

interest in basketball," my dad said.

"I didn't know either until Frankie and Ashley said they had been picked for the team."

"How's your shooting?" my dad asked.

"Needs work."

"How's your dribbling?"

"Needs work."

"How's your passing?"

"Never heard of it."

"It's when you assist another player by passing the ball so he or she can shoot," Emily said. "Everyone knows that. Even Katherine."

Emily's pet iguana, Katherine, who sits on her shoulder during dinner, whipped her tongue out and hissed at me.

"No one wants to hear from you," I snapped. "You didn't make the team."

"Do not take that tone of voice with Katherine," Emily said. "She's very sensitive."

"Awww . . . what's going to happen?" I said, faking a nice tone of voice. "Is she going to cry when she's spitting up lettuce balls?"

"For your information, Katherine digests her lettuce very well," Emily snapped.

"All right, you two," my dad said. "That's enough. Hank, after dinner I'll take you downstairs to the basement courtyard and give you some basketball pointers."

"Great idea, Dad, but there's no basketball hoop in the courtyard."

"Leave it to your creative dad," he said.

"Okay," I said, even though I had no idea what he was talking about.

"I didn't know you played basketball, Stanley," my mom said.

My dad kind of puffed up his chest. "I was a pretty fair player in my day. They called me Dr. Dunk."

"Wow, Dad," I said. "I didn't know you were a doctor, too."

"That was his nickname, you muffin head," Emily said, "because Dad scored a lot of points."

"I think you boys

will have fun playing basketball together," my mom said.

I wasn't sure. My dad can get really impatient when he's trying to teach me a game. Last week, he was trying to teach me how to play Scrabble, which is not a good game for me since I can't spell. I tried to explain to him that he could roll his eyes at me all he wanted, but it wasn't going to help me be a better speller.

My dad suggested we skip dessert and go right downstairs to practice. That was okay with me, since my mom is into making super healthy, semi-disgusting desserts. That night it was tomato soup cupcakes with blueberries.

I grabbed our basketball, and we took the elevator down to the basement. We walked through the laundry room and out the back door to the courtyard. It's a cement square surrounded on all four sides by our ten-floor apartment building. My dad reached into a grocery bag he was carrying and pulled out two wire hangers. He twisted them together, then bent them into a circle and hung them up on a nail that was sticking out of the brick.

"This is called using your head," my dad said, pointing to his homemade basket. "Now let's

practice using your hands. Take
your first shot."

I held the ball in my hands and
took aim. Just as I was about
to let it go, I heard a noise from
Mrs. Park's apartment. It sounded
like a teakettle going off. I turned
to follow the noise, and the ball
went sideways. It never even came
close to the basket.

My dad shook his head.

"You need to focus," he said.
"Concentrate. Keep your eyes on
where you want the ball to go.
Understand?"

"Completely, Dad," I said.

I picked up the ball and took aim
again. This time, I stared as hard as
I could at the basket—until a fat

gray pigeon swooped down from a
windowsill. I saw it from the corner
of my eye just as I let go of the
ball. Once again—you guessed it—
I shot a total air ball.

I could see the
frustration building up in my dad.

"Let's give shooting a rest,"
he said with a sigh. "Let me see
you dribble."

I picked up the ball and dribbled around the courtyard. At least, I tried to. It's a good thing there were four walls around me. Otherwise the ball would have rolled into the Hudson River.

Finally, we got to passing.

"Okay," my dad said. "I'll pass to you, and as soon as you catch it, pass it back to me. Step forward to meet the ball."

He threw me the ball, and it landed on my chest, but I held on to it. Then I threw it back to him, which wasn't easy, because he was moving all around the courtyard. We must have passed the ball between us five or six times in a row.

"Hey," I said, stopping to catch my breath. "I'm really good at passing. That makes me feel great."

"Don't get overconfident," my dad said. "What you need is game time. There's no better way to learn the game."

"I'll never get game time," I explained. "I'm just a substitute. Ms. Adolf doesn't want to put me in."

"We'll see about that," my dad said. "No son of mine just sits on the bench. Tomorrow, I'm going to school to have a chat with this Ms. Adolf."

"That's not such a good idea, Dad. Ms. Adolf is not very chatty."

"I'm going to ask her to put you in the game," my dad said. "All you have to do is hustle more and you'll get better. But you can't hustle without the opportunity."

Every muscle in my body froze at the idea of my dad telling Ms. Adolf to put me in the game. Number one: Ms. Adolf doesn't like to be told what to do. Number two: Did I mention Ms. Adolf doesn't like to be told what to do? And number three: Ms. Adolf doesn't like me. And if you put those three things together, it meant only one thing.

Tomorrow was going to be a disaster.

CHAPTER 6

The next day, school seemed
to drag on even more than usual.
We had a spelling test. I got
three words out of ten right,
and two of those were my name.
I had to give an oral report on
parakeets, but my brain was so
busy thinking about basketball
practice that I forgot to mention
that parakeets are birds. Luckily,
I did remember to mention that
they have beaks and wings.

After school, Frankie, Ashley,

and I ran all the way to the gym. Ms. Adolf was already standing at the entrance, clipboard in hand.

"See how prompt we are, Ms. Adolf?" I said with my best grin.

"There is no need for you to celebrate what is your responsibility," the old sourpuss said. You'd think she could come up with a little tiny smile, even a twitch of her upper lip. But noooooooooooooooo, all she said was, "Practice begins now."

The other kids arrived, and we spent the first few minutes warming up together on the court. I loved the squeaky sound our sneakers made against the polished wooden floor. I loved the echo of the ball

bouncing on the court. I loved
passing the ball and watching
everyone take a shot. I was having
so much fun, I didn't even get
nervous when Ryan Shimozato
passed me the ball and it was
my turn to shoot. It didn't go in,
but the ball actually touched the
backboard.

"Why don't you try shooting
with your eyes open, Zipper Butt,"
Nick McKelty shouted from across
the court.

"Because if my eyes were open, I'd have to see you," I shouted back to him.

The big creep had no comeback for that. It feels really good to put a bully in his place. But the good feeling didn't last long. It ended when I saw my dad walk into the gym, wearing his street shoes, which left a trail of black scuff marks all over the floor.

Ms. Adolf spoke to him before I had a chance to stop him.

"Pardon me," she said, "but parents are not invited to practice. You may come to the game on Friday."

"That's what I want to talk to you about," my dad said. "It will only take a moment of your time."

I closed my eyes and wished that I could fly. I would fly to Iceland and stay there until my father left.

"I practiced with my son, Hank, last night," my dad said, "and I saw major improvement."

"I have yet to see any improvement," she answered.

"I believe Hank will surprise

you," my dad went on, "if you just let him play. People can't improve unless you give them a chance."

"Mr. Zipzer, the point is, we are trying to create a winning team, not a losing one."

I was so embarrassed! I had to stop this conversation any way I could. I ran over to my dad and took him by the arm.

"Thanks for stopping by, Dad," I said, leading him toward the door. "Be sure and tell Mom I said hi."

I held the door open for him, but he didn't leave. Instead he stopped, turned to Ms. Adolf, and gave her his grumpy stare. I know that stare very well, because I get it every report-card day. And every left-my-homework-at-school day. And every forgot-to-make-my-bed day.

But Ms. Adolf didn't care. She just stared right back at him. That woman could stare down a snorting moose.

"Bye, Dad," I said, practically shutting the door in his face.

As soon as the door was closed, I ran back to Ms. Adolf. Like I said, she is not a person who likes being told what to do,

and I knew my dad's little visit
had probably made her mad. I was
right. By the time I reached her,
you could almost see the steam
shooting out of her ears.

"My dad loves to kid around,"
I said, before she could say one
word. "That part about letting me
play was just a joke. You don't
have to do that."

"Let's see just how improved
you are," she said. "Please join
your teammates for a passing and
shooting drill."

Each person had to pass the
ball to another team member,
who then got to take a shot
at the basket. We went around
and around the circle. Each time

I got to shoot, I missed the
basket entirely, and felt worse
and worse. I noticed Ms. Adolf
shaking her head, and it was
definitely not in the up and down
direction. Side to side is not the
kind of shake you want.

Frankie and Ashley were good
shooters, but Heather Payne was
amazing. She's so tall that when
she jumped and lifted her arms, she

could almost touch the bottom of the basketball net. But she was having trouble catching the passes from Nick McKelty. He threw the ball so hard that it smacked her in the belly and knocked the breath out of her.

"Here, Hank," she said, throwing the ball to me after she'd made a shot. "You pass it. My belly can't take another McKelty toss."

I caught the ball, dribbled a couple of times, and then passed to Heather. She caught it, spun around, and made a perfect basket.

"Wow," she said. "You're great at passing. That was an amazing assist."

I turned to Ms. Adolf as fast

as I could, to make sure she had seen that. And of course, she hadn't. She had her nose buried in her clipboard, no doubt making a note that I was the worst player on the team.

At the end of our drill, Ms. Adolf called the team together.

"In preparation for our game on Friday, I have ordered special team jerseys for you," she said. "As you'll notice, each has a number."

Oh boy. A team jersey with my own number on it. My lucky number is five. I hoped I'd get that number on my jersey. This was going to be so great.

She pulled the jerseys out of a box. They were blue with white numbers on the back. That was cool because blue and white are our school colors.

"Frankie Townsend, number 22," she called. Frankie went up and got his jersey.

"Ashley Wong!" she said. "Number 15." Ashley picked up her jersey and did a happy fist pump.

One by one, each member's name was called. Shimozato, number 7. Sperling, number 9. Patel, number 30.

At last, she had called everyone but me. That was okay. For a great moment like this, I could wait. I stood there proudly.

"Hank Zipzer," she said. I walked up to her. "Unfortunately, I ordered the jerseys before Principal Love suggested that you be on the team. Therefore, I don't have a jersey for you. However, I was able to locate a T-shirt left over from last year's team. It's number 13."

"But 13 is an unlucky number, isn't it?" I asked.

"Perhaps that's why it was left over from last year," she said. "In any case, it's all we have. It might be a bit large, but I trust you can make it work."

"But this T-shirt doesn't look like everybody else's," I said.

"Let's be honest, Henry," she said. "It doesn't really matter, since you won't be on the court during the game."

I took the T-shirt without looking at it. Even though I was embarrassed, I tried to smile to cover it up, but I couldn't make myself.

"Everyone put on your jerseys for a team picture," Ms. Adolf said.

I slipped the T-shirt over my head. It came down below my knees. I wanted to run away. I sure didn't want to be in the picture wearing that thing.

Suddenly, Frankie and Ashley were there by my side. They know me so well.

"Come on, Zip," Frankie said. "I feel like standing in the back row."

"Me too," said Ashley. "Let's go."

So we took the team picture. If you looked at it quickly, you might not notice that I was the only one without my own team jersey.

But I noticed.

CHAPTER 7

My grandfather, Papa Pete, picked us up from school after practice.

"How come Dad didn't wait around to walk us home?" I asked him.

"He had to go pick up some doggy treats for Cheerio. You know how grumpy that little puppy gets when he rolls over and there's no biscuit for him."

We left school and headed down 78th Street toward Broadway. "So how are my favorite basketball players?" Papa Pete asked as we walked.

"Not so good," I answered.

"Ms. Adolf didn't have a team jersey for Hank," Frankie explained.

"It's not about the uniform, Hankie," Papa Pete said, giving my shoulder a squeeze. "Basketball is about having fun and playing your best."

"Well, it's not fun when you play like me," I said. "I couldn't put a ball in the basket if it were as big as the ocean."

"Maybe you're not the best shooter in the world," Ashley said to me, "but you can sure pass the ball."

"It takes all kinds of skills

to make a team," Papa Pete said. "Take Larry Green on my bowling team, the Chopped Livers. He has never thrown a strike in all of our games. But he brings homemade doughnuts, and that keeps us all happy."

"I didn't even know doughnuts could be homemade," Frankie said.

"Someone has to make them," Papa Pete answered with a grin. "They don't grow on trees."

Frankie and Ashley burst out laughing, but not me. I was still feeling down in the dumps. Of course, Papa Pete noticed right away.

"I have an idea," he said. "Let's stop at Harvey's and get ourselves a slice of pizza. My treat."

The pizza cheered me up a
little. It's hard to feel too terrible
when pepperoni is involved. But
by the time I got home to our
apartment, I was feeling bad again.
It didn't help that I had to show
my dad the big blue T-shirt.

"This isn't much of a jersey,"
he said. "Is this what all the kids
are wearing?"

"I was the last picked, and they
ran out of the real ones," I answered.

"Looks like I'm going to have to have another little chat with Ms. Adolf," my dad said.

"I hope it goes better than the last one," I said.

I was headed to my room when Emily called out, "By the way, Hank, someone named Heather Payne called for you. She's a girl."

"I know, Emily," I said. "She's in my class."

"Your new girlfriend left her number."

"She's not my girlfriend, Emily. She happens to be a girl who is a friend."

That wasn't actually true. I had never hung out with Heather Payne. She had never called me before.

I wondered what she wanted to talk about. I went into the living room, picked up the phone, and dialed her number.

"Hello. Harry's Haircuts," said a voice on the other end of the phone. "You grow it, we snip it."

"May I please speak with Heather Payne?"

"Never heard of her, kiddo. You got the wrong number."

Oh no. It happened again. Every time I try to dial the phone, I press the wrong numbers. Actually, they're the right numbers, they're just in the wrong order. My eyes are looking at the numbers, but my brain mixes them all up. I tried again, pressing each number slowly and carefully.

"Hello," a voice said. I breathed a sigh of relief. It was Heather Payne.

"Hi, Heather. It's Hank. I'm calling you back."

"Yes, I know," she said. "I hear your voice."

We were both silent for a few long seconds, then—thank goodness—Heather began to talk.

"Frankie and Ashley suggested that maybe we could all get

together in your courtyard tomorrow after basketball practice," she said.

"How come?" I asked.

"Well, we were talking about how good you are at passing the ball," she said.

"You were talking about me?"

"Yes. And I have an idea about how you could help us win the game. I think you might just be our Secret Weapon."

Me? A secret weapon? Wow, that sounded great.

"I'm not sure it will work," Heather said, "but it's worth a try. Are you in for tomorrow after practice?"

"In? I'm in like Flynn. I'm in like grin. I'm in like we're going to win!"

"You're very good at rhyming,"

Heather said. "Listen, I have to go and do my subtraction worksheet. See you tomorrow."

I hung up the phone and felt pretty good . . . until I realized that I had the same subtraction worksheet. All those numbers on the page make my brain feel like mashed potatoes with no gravy.

The next day at school, all I could think about was how I might get to be the Secret Weapon. When Ms. Flowers asked me to name the three main cloud types, I didn't even hear her at first.

"Hank," Ms. Flowers said. "Are you listening? Or is your head in the clouds?"

Of course, that gave Nick McKelty a chance to shoot off his mouth.

"Zipper Teeth's head is always in the clouds," he said. "You should see him on the basketball court. He can't focus on anything."

That made me want to be the Secret Weapon even more. I'm sorry to say this, but I was super happy when Ms. Flowers made Nick McKelty write "I will not be rude" ten times in his notebook.

Our after-school practice was just like the day before—a total disaster. Ms. Adolf was especially nervous, since it was our last practice before the big game. You don't want to be around her any time, but when she's nervous, she blows her whistle after every word.

My ears were still ringing from her whistle when Frankie, Ashley, and I walked into my apartment.

"I put out a snack for you kids," my mom said. "Some cheese and crackers."

"Who wants to eat knees and smackers?" I asked.

"Hank, I said cheese and crackers. What's wrong with your ears?"

"I have whistle-itis," I said.

But I couldn't finish my explanation, because just then Heather Payne arrived at our front door. She was carrying a basketball and wearing her team jersey.

"Hi, Heather," my mom said. "Come in and help yourself to a snack. You kids are going to need an energy boost before your basketball workout."

"Thanks, Mrs. Zipzer," Heather Payne said. "But I just had a slice of pizza with my mom."

Frankie and Ashley dived in, making cheese and cracker sandwiches.

I didn't have any, though. My stomach was all jumbled up. It talks to me sometimes when it's nervous. This time it was saying, "Don't send any Swiss cheese down here. I'm still working on that bean burrito you had for lunch."

The truth is, it wasn't only my stomach that was nervous. It was all of me. My entire basketball career at PS 87 depended on whether or not I could become the second grade's Secret Weapon.

I was about to find out.

CHAPTER 8

We took the elevator down
to the basement. Just before the
door closed, Mrs. Fink, who lives
across the hall from my family,
stuck her foot in. It was wearing
a bunny slipper with floppy ears.
That's Mrs. Fink for you.

"Hold the elevator, kids,"
she said. "I'm going down to the
laundry room."

"Hi, Mrs. Fink," we all said as
she got in. I noticed that her giant
pink robe was on the top of her

laundry basket. She wears it every day. I had no idea she had any other clothes. But there she was, in a giant green robe with little purple dogs on it.

"I like your robe," I said as I pressed *B* for basement. "The little dogs on it remind me of our puppy, Cheerio."

"Except Cheerio's not purple," Ashley commented.

"He would be if he rolled in grape juice," Frankie said.

We all laughed, except for Heather. She may be tall and have a great hook shot, but she's not big on a sense of humor.

When the elevator doors opened in the basement, we headed to the laundry room. Mrs. Fink stopped at the washing machine, and we went to the door that led to the courtyard outside.

Without a word, Heather passed me the basketball. I wasn't ready, and the ball whizzed right by me.

"First rule, Hank," Frankie said. "You have to stay alert. You never know when the ball is coming your way."

I chased the ball down and started to dribble it back to Heather. It bounced on my foot and took a sharp left turn to nowhere.

"Second rule, Hank," Frankie said. "Never dribble the ball. Secret Weapons don't dribble."

"Then what do they do?" I asked.

"What you do best," Heather said. "Pass."

I shook my head. I didn't understand what they were talking about.

"Here's our plan," Heather said, pulling us all into a close circle. "Hank, you stay down by the basket and we'll get the ball to you."

"But everyone on the other team will see me just waiting by the basket."

"Trust me," Frankie said. "Everyone on the court is watching the ball. That's where their attention is."

"As soon as you get the ball in your hands," Heather said, "you pass it to me. You've got to be quick—quick as a whip."

"I can do that," I said. "Then what?"

"Then I shoot," Heather said. "Before the other team even knows what happened, we've scored."

"Let's try it out," Ashley suggested. "Secret Weapon, take your position!"

I walked over to the wire
basket that my dad had made for
our practice. I just stood there,
watching the others dribble and
pass around the courtyard. My
eyes never left the ball as it
moved from Heather to Ashley
to Frankie. Suddenly, Frankie
passed the ball to me with the
speed of a rocket. My first

thought was to duck, but I didn't.
I put my arms out and caught
that ball in midair. It was barely
in my hands when I pivoted and
passed the ball directly to
Heather. She caught it, just
as we'd planned, and made
the basket.

   Wow! We all high-fived about
ten times in a row.

"Let's do it again," I said. "My grandpa always says practice makes perfect."

I took my position by the basket and waited for the ball to come to me. This time, Ashley passed it. Just as I was about to catch it, Mrs. Fink stuck her head around the laundry-room door.

"Have fun, kids," she shouted. "When you're done, come up for a slice of my homemade marble cake."

Here's a basketball tip. It may never come up for you, but it sure did for me. You can't catch a pass if you're listening to Mrs. Fink. You're welcome.

"We've got to keep at it," Frankie said. "Pay attention, Zip.

Keep your mind in the game."

"And don't take your eye off the ball," Ashley said.

We ran through the drill over and over until it was starting to get dark. By the time we quit, we had it down perfectly. I had become, really and truly, the Secret Weapon.

We waited in the lobby for Heather's mom to come pick her up.

"Great practice," Heather said, pumping her fist as she left. "We're ready for the big game tomorrow. Go team."

I was so happy. I've never been good at sports, so being part of this team was the best feeling ever.

"We're going to win for sure tomorrow," I said. "We'll get that trophy, no problem."

"Well, there actually is one little problem," Frankie said. "Which actually isn't so little."

"What's that?"

"We have to get Ms. Adolf to put you in the game."

"Yeah," Ashley agreed. "A secret weapon doesn't do any good sitting on the bench."

They had a point. Why hadn't we thought about that?

My head dropped. My

shoulders dropped. My hopes dropped. I felt like a balloon that someone stuck a pin in.

How were we ever going to get Ms. Adolf to put me in the game?

CHAPTER 9

FOUR WAYS WE COULD GET MS. ADOLF TO PUT ME IN THE GAME

BY HANK ZIPZER

1. I could scare her into it. But with what? I could wear a zombie mask and tell her I'm going to eat her for lunch if she doesn't put me in.

2. We could get rid of her. But how? I could go on the school loudspeaker and announce that her pet cat, Fang, needs her at home to take care of a kitty-litter emergency.

3. I could give her something she's always wanted. But what? I could let her take Emily's pet iguana, Katherine, home for the weekend. They kind of look alike. She and Katherine could have a great time hissing at each other.

4. Let's face it. I don't have a fourth idea, and none of the others are going to work. My butt is going to be glued to that bench forevermore, and that is that.

CHAPTER 10

The announcer's voice echoed all around the gym.

"Welcome back from halftime," the very grown-up-sounding voice said. Actually, it wasn't really a grown-up. It was Sammy Perez, a fifth-grader who was trying very hard to sound like the announcer for the New York Knicks.

"We have a tight score here in our yearly game," he said. "PS 87 has won the title two years in a row. Will we three-peat? PS 91 doesn't think so. They want to take the trophy back with them to their school."

"Get it done, ninety-one," the crowd chanted. "Get it done, ninety-one."

"They're on the way to doing it," Sammy said. "PS 91 is in the lead with a score of 24 points." From the bleachers, moms and dads, brothers, sisters, and grandparents waved PS 91's purple flags.

"But let's not count out our very own PS 87," he said. With that, our side of the gym cheered so loud, it made the walls shake. "We're close behind with 22 points, led by our top scorer, Heather Payne."

Everyone in the bleachers stomped their feet. I jumped up on the bench and raised both my arms over my head, and shouted at the top of my lungs.

"Eighty-seven, we're the champs!" I yelled.

Okay, so it wasn't as good a chant as the other team had, but they didn't have my Zipzer spirit.

I could see my family in the stands. My mom and dad were waving a flag with our school colors, blue and white. My grandfather, Papa Pete, was wearing his only all-blue sweat suit. Usually he wears his red one and looks like a giant strawberry. Today he looked like a giant blueberry.

I wish they could see me play, but that's never going to happen, I thought to myself as I waved to my family.

I felt someone tap me on the shoulder. It was not a friendly tap.

"Henry, this bench is not for standing on," Ms. Adolf snapped. "Your job is to sit down and watch the game."

"My real job is to be the Secret Weapon," I told her.

"There you go again, talking nonsense." With that, Ms. Adolf blew her whistle so loud that it felt like my ears were flapping back and forth like an elephant's.

I sat down on the bench in between Kim Paulson and Luke Whitman. Kim was cheering for Frankie, who was dribbling down the court. When a tall girl from the PS 91 team tried to steal the ball from him, he spun around, did a behind-the-back dribble, and got by her.

"Shoot it, Frankie!" I yelled.

He did. And he made the basket. It was now a tie game.

"Whoa," Sammy Perez said into the microphone. "Frankie Townsend ties it up!"

But then, PS 91 answered right back. They had this player named Griffin. I don't know if that was his first name or his last, but he sure could shoot. He made three baskets in a row when Nick McKelty was supposed to be guarding him. No surprise there. Griffin was fast as a cheetah, and McKelty was slow as a water buffalo. McKelty got so frustrated that he poked one of his scaly elbows right into Griffin's side.

The referee noticed and blew his whistle.

"Hey," he shouted at McKelty. "I saw that! No rough stuff."

"I didn't do anything," McKelty shouted back. "You must have been looking in the wrong direction."

"I'm looking at you," the referee said. "And I saw you elbow that player. You can't do that on my court. So now I'm going to watch you walk off this court and take a seat on the bench. You're out of the game."

"Fine!" McKelty snapped at him. "I didn't want to play, anyway."

McKelty stomped over to the bench and pushed Luke Whitman aside. He was sweating so much that when he sat down, he splashed all over me.

"Hank," Ashley called from the court. "This is your chance. Tell Ms. Adolf to put you in the game."

I jumped up off the bench.

"I can go in for McKelty," I told Ms. Adolf. "I'm ready."

"So is Luke Whitman," she said. "Luke, you're in."

Luke ran onto the court. As soon as the referee blew his whistle, Ashley passed Luke the ball. He caught it with one hand, because as always, his other hand was busy picking his nose. That kid has a major snot problem.

There seems to be no end to what he can find on the inside of his nose. You'd think he'd run out after a while. But no— there it was, a big wad on the end of his finger that he smeared all over the ball.

He passed the ball to Frankie, who let it whiz right by him.

"I'm not touching that thing," Frankie said to the referee.

The referee picked up the ball very carefully, took a handkerchief out of his pocket, and wiped the ball down.

"Here you go," he said, passing the ball to Griffin.

"I'm sorry, sir," Griffin answered. "I just can't. I'm allergic to nose slime. And what happens if he does it again?"

The referee nodded.

"You have a good point, kid," he said. "Back to the bench, son," he ordered Luke. "And get yourself some Kleenex. I'd go for the jumbo box."

"You can't take me out," Luke argued. "There's no rule that says you can't put snot on the basketball."

"There is now," the ref said. "I just wrote it."

As Luke walked over to the bench, I jumped up again, but Ms. Adolf had already signaled

Kim Paulson to go in. I sighed and sat back down.

The referee blew the whistle, and the game started up. Kim wasn't bad. She was a fast runner and actually made one basket. But then, in the middle of a play, she stopped suddenly.

"Kim," I heard Frankie say. "Get in the game."

"I'm out of breath," she said. "Everyone's running so fast. What's the rush?"

She took a scrunchie off her wrist, bent over to pull her hair up onto the top of her head, and made a ponytail. Right there in the middle of the court!

"Excuse me, young lady,"
Ms. Adolf said. "There is no
hairstyling allowed in the middle
of a basketball game."

"But my hair was looking
terrible," Kim told her. "In front
of all these people."

"Fine," said Ms. Adolf. "Then
you can go sit on the bench
until you're satisfied with your
hairstyle."

I jumped off the bench and ran over to Ms. Adolf, placing myself right in front of her. She had to put me in now. Samir wasn't there because of a family emergency, and Ryan was sick and had to stay in bed. I was the only one left.

"Now can I go in?" I asked her.

"I'm so sorry to say this," Ms. Adolf said with a deep sigh. "But yes."

There it was, my big moment. Secret Weapon, reporting for duty.

CHAPTER 11

Ms. Adolf asked Nick McKelty to take off his shirt and give it to me.

"You may wear the official team jersey," she said, handing me his sweat-soaked shirt.

As much as I hated my baggy T-shirt, the thought of wearing his stinky, soggy shirt was way worse.

"Thanks anyway," I said to Ms. Adolf. "I'd rather be kissed by an orangutan."

Before she could answer,
I ran onto the court.

"Okay, everybody huddle,"
Heather Payne said as soon as
I joined my teammates.

"Actually, I think *huddle* is
a football term," Katie Sperling
pointed out.

"Fine, then everyone clump
together," Heather said.

The whole team laughed. Even
I knew that *clump* wasn't a sports
term.

"We have to get serious here," Heather said. "It's 30 to 26. We're behind by four points. That means we have to make three more baskets to win."

"And we can't let them score again," Ashley added.

"So are we ready to launch our Secret Weapon plan?" Heather asked.

"I am, that's for sure," I said.

"Wait a minute," Katie interrupted. "What's a Secret Weapon?"

"You'll see," Frankie said, with all the confidence in the world. "Hank, take your position."

As I ran to my place down by the basket, I realized that Frankie had all the confidence in the world, but mine was dripping out my toes. I looked up at the stands, and boy, were there a lot of eyeballs staring at me. I found my family in the crowd. My dad looked worried. My mom seemed to be chewing on her fingernails. My sister was reading a book, probably her favorite, *100 Lizard Facts Everyone Should Know.* Papa Pete waved at me and mouthed "You can do it!"

I hoped he was right.

The referee blew the whistle, and the game started up again. In a great move, Frankie stole the ball as it was being passed from one PS 91 player to another. He dribbled it down the court, then fired a pass to me. It was coming fast. I planted my feet and put my arms out.

"Don't you dare drop this, Hank Zipzer," I said to myself.

I'm not sure, I might have even said it out loud. That's how hard I was concentrating.

"Don't pass it to Zipper Teeth!" I heard Nick McKelty yell from the bench.

Bam! The ball smacked me

right in the chest.
Quickly, I
wrapped my hands
around it before
it hit the floor. It
wasn't the prettiest

catch in the world, but it worked.
I pivoted and saw Heather Payne
waving her arms wildly at me. I
knew what to do. I passed her the
ball. She caught it, and in one
move, shot that ball right through
the hoop.

"Will you look at that?" Sammy
Perez shouted into the microphone.
"Hank Zipzer makes the assist.
Where did he come from?"

"That's my grandson,"
Papa Pete yelled from the

stands. "And don't you forget it!"

Frankie and Ashley ran up
and high-fived me so hard that
I nearly fell over.

"Let's do that again," Frankie
said.

And we did, once Ashley stole
the ball from the other team and
chucked it over to me. Ms. Adolf
couldn't believe what she was
seeing. She just stood by the side
of the court with her
whistle hanging off
her lower lip. She
was so shocked,
she couldn't even
blow it.

"Okay, folks, we
have a tie game on our hands,"

Sammy's voice blared. "We've got thirty-six seconds on the clock. Who's going to get that trophy? Stay tuned to find out."

Did he say "Stay tuned"? I wondered who Sammy thought he was talking to. We weren't on TV.

The coach of PS 91 had called a time out. With his team surrounding him, he was talking up a storm. I saw him point at me. That felt great, until I realized that he had figured out that I was the Secret Weapon.

Our team gathered around me.

"Okay, Hank," Ashley said. "They know that you're the Secret Weapon. That means they're going to try to stop you from getting the ball and passing it to Heather."

Ms. Adolf had joined us on the court.

"As your coach, I suggest you keep it away from Henry," she said.

"But, Ms. Adolf," Frankie argued. "Hank just helped us make two amazing baskets and tie the game."

"I heard that last week he knew all his spelling words, yet he failed his spelling test. Some people are just not good under pressure."

Oh man! I was having the best time of my life, and she

had to go and bring up spelling!

The whistle blew, and the team from **PS** 91 took the court. So did we.

At first, things were not going well. Griffin, their best player, had the ball. Frankie tried to steal it, but couldn't. Griffin dribbled down to the basket and took a shot. We all held our breath as we watched it fly through the air toward the hoop.

It looked like it was going in, until it bounced off the rim.

Ashley jumped as high as she could and grabbed it out of the air. She whipped around so fast that her glasses flew off her face. She couldn't see where to pass it, but heard Frankie's voice shouting, "Over here, Ashweena!"

She made a perfect pass. Frankie got the ball, and I raced to my Secret Weapon position just as his pass arrived. I had it! I had the ball! The clock was ticking. We had twelve seconds left in the game.

But there was one little problem. Actually, there were five big problems. All five members of the PS 91 team were racing toward me. In no time, they were in front of me, arms up, blocking me from making a pass. Out of the corner of my eye, I could see Heather waiting for the ball, but there was no way I could get it to her.

Oh wait. Yes there was.

I bent over and bounced the ball backward through my legs. That surprised the PS 91 team. No one was expecting that move, not even me!

"Heather! It's behind him!"
Frankie yelled.

Heather and I were on the
same wavelength. She darted
for the ball and grabbed it.
In one swift move, she turned
to the basket, quickly aimed, and
shot the ball.

Boom! It was a perfect
basket.

Our side of the bleachers
cheered so loud, you could
hardly hear the buzzer go off.
But it did go off.

We had won the game.

And the three-peat.

And the biggest trophy you've
ever seen.

I can't believe I'm saying this,

but I, Hank Zipzer—PS 87's
Secret Weapon—was part of
the winning team.

Wow, that was sweet.

CHAPTER 12
THREE GREAT THINGS ABOUT WINNING THAT TROPHY

BY HANK ZIPZER

1. The kindergartners all asked for our autographs. I signed mine Hank "S.W." Zipzer.

Hank
S.W.
Zipzer

2. When I was chosen by the team to put the trophy in the display case, Nick McKelty actually had to say congratulations.

PS 87

3. Ms. Adolf gave me her whistle
for doing such a good job.
Even though it's got her
cooties on it, I still kind of
like it.